Geek As

Isolation

Survival Instincts

The Perfect Gift

Never Go There

Short Horror Story Collection

By

Michelle Birbeck

Michelle Birbeck xx

Kiss kiss!

Isolation

The quiet lapping of the sea against the rocks and sand was interrupted by a shout of joy. It was quickly followed by the loud thump of the start of a random song. Chris had finally gotten the music working.

"Batteries," Tom said, glancing over his shoulder towards the fire.

"Well, I told him so, but he never listens. Has to work it out on his own."

We'd been at the beach for an hour, working our way around to this secluded place before the sea had chance to cut us off. It was in now, tight against rocks that were no longer passable by foot. Not that we planned on going anywhere. I looked at the three tents before me. Far enough away from the sea, and close enough to the sheer cliff to give us some shelter until morning. Tom and I had erected them, choosing the locale whilst the others set the fire and got the music going. Which had turned out to be more complicated than putting up tents in the dark with only one torch between us.

"There, that's about the best job we can do."

I nodded. "Think we should go help with the fire? I'd like to eat some time tonight."

Tom laughed, and I joined him. Vanessa and Julie weren't used to the outdoors. They were girls, unlike myself who apparently was more boy than anything else, despite my being a blond. They were the kind of girls who thought hair straighteners were appropriate packing for camping, and that all tents were equipped with electrical outlets.

"Yeah, come on, I'm not sure the pair of them are safe to be let loose with matches, let alone firewood and lighter fluid!"

We laughed it up on the short trip back to the non-existent fire and pounding music. At least the latter was up and running. Though uncooked burgers and raw potatoes weren't as appealing as they might sound.

"How we doing?" I asked.

Vanessa and Julie turned to look at me, and it took everything I had in me not to double over laughing. Their dark hair was framing even darker faces that were normally white. How they've gotten soot all over their faces was a mystery. Making a fire was easy! Get some kindling together, add something that burned easily, set a match, wait for it to light, and hey presto, fire.

Apparently not.

"Need a hand?" Tom's voice came out jittery. He was trying to hold back a laugh, as well.

Relief flooded their faces, and I half expected them to cry out with it. They didn't. Instead they both held up their supplies, reaching out as though they'd been offered food after starving for months.

Lighter fluid and matches were handed over, and the girls scooted back, out of the way.

"Did you bring the wet wipes?" Vanessa asked.

"In the tent."

Their comic value was one of the reasons we'd stayed friends for so long. It might have been mean for me to laugh at them as I did, but both were well aware of their bimbo status, and used it mercilessly on the opposite sex. They'd even gone so far as to try and convert me, but jeans were where I lived, and no amount of pretty shoes and sex was going to change my mind.

Besides, I did well enough on my own. Never underestimate the power of being a tomboy. Plenty of men found my being able to be one of the boys a real turn on.

Shaking my head, I turned away from Tom and his fire. Once the fire was up, we could start the party proper, but in the meantime, there were beers to be had. As well as shots for games later, mixers for the morning hangovers, and spirits for hard-core among us.

"Gimmie all your money."

I closed my eyes. "Nice try, Chris. But in case you forgot, we're alone here."

When I turned, I spotted the glint of a knife in his hands and raised my brow.

"What? I needed it to get the batteries out."

Isolation

"So it was them, then?"

"Yeah." He rubbed the back of his neck and looked down.

"Told ya so."

Slowly, he folded the knife and put it back in his pocket. A smile played on his face in the moonlight. It was almost seductive. Almost. Because I knew he had his eye on one or both of the girls. No doubt they'd end up in the same tent, or sharing the same seat, or getting right down to it in front of everyone.

His smile was lit once again in a flash that died down to a yellow glow. We both looked in the direction of Tom. The fire was going.

"Great, now we can see about some food!" Ah, Chris's second love. Food. His first being women, and his third being the gym.

We ambled towards the fire, the heat form it making a pleasant bubble around the growing flames.

"Jackets can go on now," Tom told us as we approached. "I'd get the girls to get them, but they're busy cleaning up."

"Just how *did* they get soot all over their faces?"

"Same way they got their eyebrows singed off last time. They're talented."

That was one way of putting it. On the last of our semi-annual get togethers, the girls had singed their eyebrows, and Julie had burned her right hand. They'd been in charge of setting up the tents. Which apparently included fancy new lamps they'd found.

"They've got battery operated lights this year, right?"

Chris nodded.

"Good. 'Cause there's no getting out now until first light."

"I'll go get the spuds."

As Tom headed off for the potatoes, Chris and I settled in next to the cooler. Best seats in the house. Or on the beach as the case was.

Celebrating the start of summer with the ceremonial fire starting, drinking, and camping was the way we'd done things since we all met about four years ago at the end of college. How we'd gone through three years at the same school and missed each other was another mystery, but there we were at the end, celebrating the summer and our graduation. None of us knew each other, but we'd sat up around the fire until the first light of dawn drowned out the burning of college books and papers. Every six months since, we'd done the same. It had been an end to a part of our lives, and a start to the rest of them.

The scream that shattered the darkness had me dropping the bottle in my hands. Both Chris and I turned towards the sound, expecting it to be a prank or Tom chasing one of the girls, but he was half way back to the fire, laden down with potatoes.

And running out after him was Vanessa, still screaming.

What the hell?

Sat, frozen to the spot, it wasn't until she got close to the light of the fire that I saw the darkness spread on her hands. She was holding them in front of her, looking from one to the other as she ran, not looking where she was going.

Tom dropped the spuds, and raced towards her, tackling her to the ground before she hit the fire. Both Chris and I were too stunned to do anything.

She stumbled by the fire, jolting up from our stupor.

"Vanessa!" The name was on all of our lips. Quickly followed by "What happened?" "Is that blood?" and "Where's Julie?"

When Vanessa finally opened her mouth and started to speak, it came out jilted and quiet. "She went down to the water. We didn't bring the wet wipes, so I gave her a towel. She didn't come back, so I went after her. She… She was on the floor. I thought she was joking. B-but when I t-turned her over there was… Oh, God! The blood! It was everywhere!"

Her voice was shrill in the end, the words merging together as she curled in on herself. Her hands were as far away as possible. They were shaking, fingers spread apart as though she didn't want to feel the blood of her friend between them.

I rose to my feet and started towards the waterline.

"Where are you going?" Tom asked, placing a restraining hand on my arm.

I shrugged him off. "Someone's got to go see what happened."

"Then I'm coming with you!"

Isolation

"Fine." I didn't want to be on my own, anyway.

Tom grabbed a torch, and we left Chris looking after Vanessa. Together we eased our way down to the water, shining the light far ahead of us. Neither of us wanted to trip over the body of our friend.

"You're shaking," Tom said.

I looked down at my hands, and yes, they were trembling. It wasn't cold out, and the fine tremor had nothing to do with the mild sea breeze that accompanied our plans. It had everything to do with the sound of that scream running through my mind again and again. I'd never heard anything like it, and just the memory of it turned my insides cold.

When I closed my eyes, I hoped the shaking would stop, the darkness of my lids covering everything we were about to see and had already heard. But all it did was root me to the spot. Fear froze me, taking hold of me as sure as if I was held in a tight vice.

Why had I been the one to say we needed to go see what had happened?

An arm around my waist made me gasp.

"Hey, it's just me," Tom whispered. "You okay?"

I nodded, not trusting my voice.

"You want me to go alone?"

"No, no, we should stick together." My words may have been full of bravado, but the shake in my voice gave me away.

We set off again, Tom's arm still wrapped around my waist. We'd never been attracted to each other, but it was nice to have him there, to know that no matter what we saw, there was something good and solid and so very real right next to me.

And that was the only thing that stopped me stumbling and falling face first into the rocks. Ones covered in blood.

It was shiny and red in the light of the torch, the LED bulbs giving it a bluish tinge that reminded me of a Magpie.

Oh, shit!

Julie hadn't just slipped and fallen, only to die. She'd crawled first, leaving a trail of red along the rocks in her wake.

"Where is she?" I whispered, unable to stand the sound of my voice even then.

Tom swung the light wildly, tracing the blood with shaky hands. "There."

The beam landed on her feet. She wasn't moving, and neither were we. Too shocked to do much more than stand, we stayed where we were, eyes following the light of the torch, minds unable to comprehend what we were seeing.

Silence filled the void our footsteps had occupied. Not even the close swelling and receding of the ocean reached my ears as I stared along the beam of light.

"Stay here." Tom's voice made me jump.

I didn't protest as he pulled out his phone and clicked on its light. He handed me the torch and started in the direction of Julie. Keeping the light trained on her feet as steadily as possible, I tried not to see him turning her over, tried not to let the moonlight fill in the details that would surely haunt me. But it was all for nothing. His phone cast a glow on Julie that my eyes couldn't fail to register.

Sticking out of the middle of her chest was a tent peg. The gleaming silver a bright contrast against her blood soaked shirt.

How… Even in my mind I couldn't finish the sentence.

"She's dead." Tom's whispered voice floated across the rocks, but as it landed on my ears, I couldn't fully understand the meaning behind his words.

Sure, I knew what he'd said. But this was *Julie!* I'd laughed at her so often as she and Vanessa tottered around on heels, flirting with anything that had three legs. We'd laughed together when I'd tried it and fallen flat on my face after just one step.

She couldn't be gone!

Vanessa would be devastated.

"Hey, hey, come here!"

Tom engulfed me in his arms, turning me away from the sight. Not that it mattered. The sight of that tent peg would forever haunt me.

My sobs were silent, muffled by Tom's jacket. They came fast and hard, and all the while he held me, rocking me slightly, murmuring words of comfort.

Isolation

It was a while before I gathered myself enough to speak. "We should get back."

Tom just nodded and offered me a hand up off the floor.

When had I ended up on the floor?

Everything was a bit of a blur as we walked back to the fire, me snuggled against Tom's chest, him leading the way. I was trying to find the words to say to Vanessa, but everything that I came up with sounded stupid.

How could I tell her that her best friend was lying dead on the rocks? And that we couldn't do anything until morning because there was no way out and no phone signal without climbing a sheer cliff face. Even then, what would happen? The coastguard would send the helicopter, they'd take us all out of here... but we'd still be left missing a friend.

Turned out, I didn't need to say anything. She was still lying by the fire, arms outstretched. Chris was sat next to her, watching her closely, but eyes scanning the darkness every few seconds.

He whispered something to Vanessa then stood as we approached. Jogging down the beach, his face was solemn, and he kept glancing back.

"Well?"

Tom kept his answer low and to the point. "She's dead. Looks like she fell on one of the tent pegs."

"How?"

"No idea." Tom shook his head.

I just stood there in silence.

But as they continued to discuss what had happened and the how and the whys, I shrugged out of the conversation and walked up the beach to Vanessa. She didn't glance at me as I sat down next to her, placing my hand on her shoulder.

Her fingers were clean. The sight confused me for a moment. There'd been blood on them when we left, but now they were clean. Chris must have wiped the blood off. It didn't appear as though she knew, not with the way her fingers were still spread wide.

"Vanessa?" I whispered, shaking her just a little. "Hey, sweetie, you still with us?"

Her eyes shifted slowly to look at me, then went right back to staring at her fingers.

Had she tried to save her friend's life? Was that how the blood had gotten under her nails and on her face? Or had she stumbled and fell in the dark?

I didn't want to know. What I wanted was for it to be dawn so we could get to the path and get high enough for our phones to work. What I wanted was to wake up and find that this was all just a drunken nightmare and I'd really partied the night away and passed out in my tent.

But Julie wasn't just Vanessa's friend. She was my friend, too. And when the light of day finally freed us, we would all be leaving with the heavy loss on our shoulders.

Tom and Chris came back, taking seats around the fire. No one spoke for a while. We sat there staring at the fire, trying to ignore the reality bearing down on us.

It wasn't long before the silence turned oppressive and the crackling fire sounded as loud as gunshots.

"We going to sit like this all night?" I asked.

Sure, we weren't likely to start making small talk and drinking up a storm as we'd planned, but sitting around in silence was going to drive me insane. I only liked silence when I was on my own.

"There's no way of getting out?" Chris asked, his voice quiet and distant.

"Not unless you want to climb that cliff in the dark," Tom replied.

"Look, we're best waiting until morning, then we can send someone up, call the coast guard, and get us out of here. Even if we can climb that cliff, it'll be easier for them to find us in the morning. Which is, what? Four hours from now?" My arguments sounded reasonable to my ears, but in the back of my mind I was thinking *what if she gets cold?*

Vanessa sat up, startling me away from my thoughts.

She stayed upright for a moment, staring into the fire. Then her eyes shifted to me, but there was nothing in them. They were vacant, like a house that had been boarded up and shut down. No one home, at least not anyone the world wanted to know about.

"Vanessa?" I wanted to reach out to her, wrap her in a hug, comfort her in some way, but that empty stare made me pause.

"Will you come with me?" she asked. "I don't want to go alone."

"Go where?"

"I need to pee."

I offered her a sad smile as I rose to my feet, holding out my hand for her. She clung to me once she was upright, and I let her.

"We'll just be a minute."

Tom nodded. "Be careful."

We turned away and started down the beach. The crunching of our footsteps was our only company in the dark. My torch bobbed along in front of us, bouncing off rocks and half-dead plants clinging to life. It all brought about too many memories. The light on the rocks as Tom searched for Julie. The blood she'd left in her attempt to get to someone, anyone.

"Here?" Vanessa whispered.

"Wherever you want."

She stepped away from me slightly and looked over her shoulder. "I'll just be a second."

I watched as she wandered off down the beach a little, looking for somewhere to go. It didn't really matter where; I'd seen such things before on previous trips. Where one or more of us were too drunk to stray far from the light and warmth of the fire.

For the second time that night, a scream tore through the air. It brought my head up and made my blood run cold. Suddenly my feet were moving, eating up the ground beneath them. Others joined me, running alongside me until we were close enough that the screams drowned out our footfalls.

Coming to a stop, I turned to the side, fell to my knees, and promptly threw up everything in my stomach.

Vanessa lay on her side, screaming in what must have been agony. Something that looked a lot like a bear trap was biting through her arm and leg. Even against her dark jeans the blood was obvious. But more obvious were the traps still set around her. Three of them still splayed wide, like hungry Venus fly traps waiting for bait.

"Stay still," someone said.

"We need out of here."

"How do you expect to get her anywhere? It's not like she can swim or climb like this!"

My voice came through calmer than I'd have expected. "Can we free her?"

Whether we could get out before dawn didn't matter. If Vanessa stayed in the traps all night she'd be dead before we had chance to save her.

Time must have passed me by as I thought of how we were going to get through this night, because the next thing I heard was another almighty scream. I looked up just in time to see Chris and Tom working together to free her from the traps. They each had one in their hands, using brute strength to pry the things apart.

Where did they even come from?

It wasn't as though someone could pop on down to the corner shop and pick up a couple of traps. I didn't even know if they were available in this country. Then again, anything could be bought over the internet.

"What are they doing out here?" My whispered words went unheard as another cry filled the air.

Chris had Vanessa up in his arms, cradling her close as though the contact could somehow reverse what had happened or stop the pain she was in. The only thing that would do that was an airlift out of this place and some heavy duty pain killers. Even then it wasn't going to bring Julie back.

"Amber? We should head back. Chris is going to see if he can get one of the phones to work."

Had they discussed it? If they had, I hadn't heard.

Slowly, I rose to my feet. Tom steadied me before I realised that I was listing to one side. So much blood! And for what? Why had someone left those things there? Which in turn raised another question. *Had* Julie slipped and fell?

But more importantly, was there someone else here?

Isolation

I gripped Tom, needing to hold on to something solid, something real. The thought that there could be someone else here, on this very same beach, scared me so deeply that it was all I could do to stay on my feet.

"You okay, Amber?" Tom whispered.

I nodded.

"I've got you."

When I looked up into his eyes, they were impossibly kind and understanding. There was something else there, too. Something I'd thought I'd seen in the past but had always dismissed it.

Instead of pursuing it, I asked, "What are we going to do?"

He shrugged, the movement rocking me slightly. "We're going to go back to the fire, and we're going to take Vanessa with us. Outside that, all we can do is pray."

"Or climb."

Chris's suggestion was almost certain suicide.

"Let's get her back to the fire first, keep her warm." At least Tom had his head screwed on. "You okay to walk?"

Was I? No question I'd have to be.

Moving to stand on my own, I shuddered. Against the cold. Against the sound that ripped its way free of my friend as she was lifted. Against the images plaguing me. Against the night that was left and a dawn too far away.

Mercifully, Vanessa passed out after a few steps. Her cries ceased, her body going limp.

We passed the tents on the way, and I grabbed a couple of sleeping bags for her. Better she use them than us. We had the fire, and I doubted we'd be sleeping any time soon.

"How bad does it look?" I asked when Vanessa was laid out and wrapped up.

"Bad enough that I still think climbing's a good idea."

"And I still say it's suicide."

But Chris was right. There were no guarantees that Vanessa would make it until morning. Nothing to say we were on our own here or at the mercy of someone we'd yet to see.

But still… if Chris slipped, just once. It was nothing but rocks to break his fall, and then another of my friends would be dead, waiting on the shore for a morning they'd never see.

I interrupted their continued discussion with a quiet voice. "Is there anywhere with a soft landing? Just in case?"

Both turned harsh stares my way, as though I'd came right out and told them to get off their asses and get climbing. I didn't want either of them to have to do it, but with Vanessa passed out, her arm and leg a tangled mess, and Julie still on the rocks with vacant eyes, what choice did we have?

Chris slapped his knees and got to his feet. "Right. I'm the best climber out of us, so let's see what we can do." All the bravado in his words couldn't hide the shake in them.

"I'll stay with her," I offered. It was better to have someone here in case she woke up.

Tom's hand landed on my shoulder. The weight was warm and welcome. "We'll not be far."

A short, hysterical squeak of a laugh escaped me. "Not like there's far to go."

They walked off into the dark, far enough that all I could see was the bobbing of their light. Placing my head in my hands, I leaned forward, hoping the dark would be a welcome relief from the gore. It was. For a moment.

Then Vanessa moaned and it all came rushing back to me.

Fear filled me just as sure as if I'd eaten so much I couldn't eat any more. I was sick to the stomach with it. If someone was out to get us, then here I was, all on my own, with a roaring fire as bright as any beacon.

Frantically, I looked around, searching for something I could use as a weapon.

Wood. Plenty of sturdy pieces of wood piled up next to one of the chairs, ready to go on the fire.

It'd be just like swinging a bat.

Except, I'd never killed anyone before. Save for the occasional fly and spider, I'd never killed anything. But I *thought* I could kill another

Isolation

human being if my life depended on it. So I grabbed a piece of wood, weighed it in my hands as though I knew what I was doing, and sat back down with it resting across my knees.

I think I drifted off for a moment, though how I managed it I have no idea. One moment I was sat staring at the fire, glancing at Vanessa every few seconds, the next I was coming awake, on my feet, with my weapon in my hands.

Tom was racing towards me, shouting.

"Amber! Amber!" He skidded to a stop in front of me. "Oh, thank goodness!"

"What happened?" Adrenaline was coursing through me, making everything seem sharp and focused, despite having been asleep.

"It was Chris!"

I blinked. Once. Twice. Maybe a third time. "I'm sorry, what?"

"It was him!" He griped my shoulders tightly, shaking me a little. "He did it!"

Everything around me became like a slow motions movie screen. Tom was still throwing around crazy words about Chris. The fire was crackling slowly, its warmth pleasant against my bare skin. And somewhere in the back of my mind words were easing into place, like a snow storm settling, revealing a landscape in the whiteout.

Yet the scene before me was of an alien world.

"Chris did what?"

"He *killed* Julie. He tried to kill *me*!"

The blinking thing happened again. Once, twice, another couple of times as the sternness in Tom's voice sank in. Chris. My friend Chris. Who I'd known for years, since the end of college. Who I'd almost slept with on more than a couple of occasions...

"But *why?*" Surely he had no reason to want any of us dead. And if he did, then what of all the other times we'd come to the beach? There was that one time when a spring tide had snuck up on us and washed out the only safe path for getting back. We'd been stranded for another six or so hours waiting on the tide to go out. And what about every time we came to this place? Along that narrow path with rocks on one side and no way of climbing out on the other. It was

13

low enough, sure, but one slip at the wrong time and the tide would bash someone against the rocks with little they could do about it.

"I want to see him."

What a way that was to get Tom's attention and make him stop talking. Not that I'd heard anything he said.

"I took care of him."

"I want to see him." Because of all the things I believed in, Chris being a killer was not one of them.

Tom squeezed my shoulders again. "Amber, I don't think that's a good idea."

"Why?"

"Because we were part way up the cliff when he tried to push me off."

"And?"

"I had no choice."

I eyed him carefully, trying to make sense of his words. "What did you do?"

"Amber, we were part way up the cliff. He tried to push me off. What do you think I did?"

"I still want to see him."

"For god's sake, why!"

"Because if he was really after us, then I want to make sure he's dead. That a good enough reason?"

He shook his head a little, a small hint of a smile playing at the corner of his lips. "You can be a cold hearted bitch sometimes."

"Did you check? Because if he really is… *was* behind this, then I don't want him sneaking up on me because we didn't check."

"Fair point."

He turned and strode across the shale and sand, expecting me to follow. And I did.

Following the bobbing light in silence, I kept glancing at Tom. He seemed shaken, his hands making the light jump more than normal.

Our feet crunching their way across the beach sounded loud in the dark. The night seemed so dense, as though it was engulfing everything that wasn't bathed in light. My breathing came short and fast, making me remember why I was here, why I was following Tom to the base of the cliff.

"Here," Tom said over his shoulder.

The light was shining on a crumpled pile of clothing. Tom held it out for me, giving me the chance to back away, to leave the body as it was. But I had to check.

Take a deep breath, I told myself. *Just get it over with.*

I grabbed the torch, gripping it in my hands as though it was a life raft, an anchor into a world where everyone was still alive. One foot in front of the other, determined steps. Kneel down on the rocks, shards biting into my knee through my jeans. A shaking hand reaching out, finding a neck in the pile of clothes, searching it for a pulse, any sign of life.

Nothing.

With a deep sigh, I straightened out, turned my back on Chris's body, and returned to Tom. But it wasn't until I was next to him, leaning into his side, that I could fully come back to my own body and take stock of what was happening.

"How long until we can get out?"

"A couple of hours. I can climb if you want."

I shook my head. "No. We should wait until the tide goes out."

Vanessa was still out when we got back to the fire. The potatoes were still on the ground somewhere, little bundles of what our night might have been, and what it now was.

When I knelt next to her, she stirred a little, but even to my untrained eyes the sooner she got help, the better.

"What do we do then?" I asked quietly.

"Wait, then hike out and call for help."

I nodded, it was all the response I could muster.

Taking a seat next to Vanessa, we fell into silence. There was nothing to say, not really. Chris was dead. We were safe. Nothing could be done for Julie, and the best we could do for Vanessa was not get ourselves killed in trying to get out before dawn.

But as the hours ticked away, minutes dragging on, Vanessa's breathing changed, coming in quicker, shorter gasps. Time seemed to

15

have two different speeds for us. One for Tom and me, slow and determined. And one for Vanessa, speeding up the process of her death whilst we sat still, unable to do anything.

But eventually the two speeds evened out, and the first light of dawn turned the sky a colour more blue than black. The lapping of the ocean faded slightly, and when I glanced towards the sea, it was further out than it had been.

"Do you think we can try now?" I asked.

"We can look."

Before we left, I leaned in close to Vanessa. "Hang on, honey, we'll get help as soon as we can."

"Got your phone?"

"Yeah, you?"

"Yeah."

Better to have both than none.

There seemed little point in taking anything with us, so we left it there. The tents that hadn't been used, fire still warm enough to benefit Vanessa, chairs scattered about. We were coming back, no doubt. Everyone would have questions.

We kept an eye on the edge as we started up the path. It wouldn't do anyone any good if we were to fall now.

But as we slowly walked the path back to the cars, to phone service, and to the start of a long day, one thing was bothering me. Chris had been the one to do it, to make a good night into hell, but why? What had possessed him to kill?

The more I thought about it, putting one foot in front of the other, the more other little things occurred to me. Hadn't Chris been with me when Julie had been killed? I could swear we'd been sat together next to the fire when her scream had filled the air.

Tom nudged me a little, jolting me from my thoughts. "What you thinking about?"

I glanced up at him, seeing his pleasant smile and hearing the light tone in his voice, and something clicked into place.

His smile grew and grew until he was positively grinning. Chris *had* been with me when Julie had been killed. So unless Vanessa had killed

Isolation

her friend and maimed herself, there were only two other people who could have done it.

And I hadn't killed anyone.

"Why?" The word barely made it passed my gritted teeth.

Tom narrowed his eyes at me. "You really don't know?"

I tried to step away from him, only to find myself at the edge of the cliff. "Know? You *killed* our friends! Why would I know anything about it!"

"Because I did it for you."

"What?"

He stepped forward, grabbing my shoulders. "With them out of the way, we can be together."

Still it made no sense. I understood his words, and thought I knew what he was trying to say. The little looks every so often and the eagerness to stay close all clicked quite happily into place in my mind, but it made no sense. Surely it was all just him wanting to be close to a friend? The same as I wanted to be close to him, because I liked him, and he meant something to me.

Clearly not as much as he thought I meant to him.

"Tom," I said slowly, "I don't think of you like that. I never have."

For a moment I thought he was going to throw me off the cliff and be done with it. But instead he pulled me against him, wrapping his arms around me and starting whispering soothing words. I ignored them as best I could, subtly shifting my feet until he had to move with me or lose his balance. So far gone in his ramblings about me being delusional and not needing to worry because we were going to have a fantastic life together, he didn't notice that I'd gotten us completely turned around.

No longer was my back to the cliff, with only air between me and death. Now he was there, I just needed to get him off me.

"Tom," I said sternly, "it's not going to be like that. We are not going to have a life together. You killed my friends, murdered them. How can you expect me to love you when you maimed Vanessa, shoved a tent peg through Julie's chest, and pushed Chris off a cliff?"

I was trying to agitate him.

Michelle Birbeck

I finished by saying, "You sicken me."

He dropped his arms and glared at me. Then took one step back…

Straight over the edge of the cliff.

Fingers scrabbled at the edge for a brief second, and then his scream carried along the wind like a breath of fresh air.

I sank to my knees, closed my eyes, and dragged out my phone.

Signal. Blessed signal.

Survival Instincts

Cool, clear skies rose above her in the depths of a never-ending autumn. A full moon hung in the air, its light filtering down through the half-bare trees, casting a silvery glow across the undergrowth. The gentle breeze made the shadows dance, casting them long and wide, making it impossible to hide in their changing darkness. Racing through the woods, Leanne was running for her life, fearfully checking over her shoulder every few seconds, eyes darting across the shifting shadows. Her footsteps were loud and harsh on the dry ground, slapping away the silence that would prevent her from being found. Her heart was racing, pounding in her chest as she fought for breath. With her life on the line, she couldn't afford to be caught, not now, not ever. If he found her, if he followed her crashing footsteps, sounding like thunder in the quiet night, then he would kill her.

If he caught her, she would die by his hands.

Leanne didn't want to die. Not *this* night, the night that was supposed to be filled with such happiness. Not this cool night in the best autumn of her whole life.

With her breathing echoing in her mind, making everything sound like the whoosh of a strong wind, Leanne pushed herself faster and faster, trying to get away. Her mind was filled with fear, consuming every part of her. She wondered often, as she glanced back again and again checking to see if she was safe, how she had got here. How she had ended up running for her life, running away from a monster.

Running from the man that she loved. The man that she was supposed to marry.

It had started out as such a normal evening. Dinner in a nice restaurant, lit with low lights and tall candles. Food served by uniformed waiters on fancy plates, with just a hint of the class that cost a small fortune. It was the perfect dinner for the perfect evening. Soft music filling the air, providing a melodious backdrop to the events that unfolded. Kyle, the man that Leanne had loved for almost a year now, had taken her there, insisting on paying the bill, and then producing a diamond ring that sparkled in the low lights. He'd slipped from the table into a kneeling pose, the ring held high.

"Will you marry me?" he asked in the sudden hush of the restaurant. His voice was like a cool winter morning when the room hadn't quite woken up, but the covers were soft and warm from a busy night. His words had slid along her skin with the promise of many nights warming those covers, and many mornings waking up together.

"Yes," she'd answered.

There'd been no hesitation. The yes that she spoke came as quietly as the music, but more determined than anything she had ever said before. It came as a commitment to the man kneeling in front of her, to the life that they would have together. To devoting her life to him.

Something Leanne feverishly wished she could go back and change.

In light of the events that had unfolded after the proposal, spreading wide like some kind of macabre flower whose petals were death not beauty, she wished she'd never met Kyle. Wished that his thick brown hair hadn't been so soft under her fingers the day he'd asked her to cut it. Leanne would have traded anything to change that day, to call in sick to her work as a hairdresser, to have been in a different place or a different time. A different *anything*.

But he'd seemed so *normal*. So *loving*. So *not* like someone who would turn around and try to kill her.

She'd seen murderers on the TV, serial killers even, but they all *looked* like the sort of people to slice you up and leave you in pieces scattered across the world for the animals to devour. Kyle... there was nothing about him that screamed 'I'm going to kill you!'

He was just the first good guy that had come along in far too long. With his soft hair and piercing brown eyes, Leanne had been smitten from the start. So when he asked for her number, after twenty minutes of small talk whilst cutting his hair, she gave it to him. Handed it over. Along with her life, though she hadn't known that at the time.

That had been a year ago. A year of dinners and dating, sharing the same bed and making love whenever the mood took them. A whole year and Leanne hadn't seen it.

She'd missed the little things that he did. The behavioural traits that seemed so normal to her, but actually marked Kyle for what he truly was: an unstable psychopath who could snap at any moment. One who had chosen what should have been the happiest moment of Leanne's life to snap and take out everything in his path. Becoming a destructive force that held no regard for the life it was about to destroy.

Darkness had already closed around her when it happened, when Kyle had snapped. Sitting in the car, looking out at the sparkling city below them, Leanne leaned into Kyle's warm embrace, only to feel the coldness that had been left behind. When she turned to him, concerned that something was wrong, she saw something in his eyes that had only been hinted at in the year before. He was sat, still as a statue, staring past her with a look of hatred in his eyes.

"Kyle?" she asked, twisting in the seat so that they were facing each other. "Kyle, what's wrong?"

When he turned his eyes to her, she flinched, backing away as far as she could in the enclosed space of the car. They'd been so cold, so dead. There was nothing left in there of the man that she loved.

Confused by his sudden mood, Leanne reached for him, wondering if she'd said something wrong, done something. She had no idea what had caused the sudden shift, no clue as to what had gone so wrong that it would cause such a reaction in him after her acceptance of his proposal...

Leanne fell to the ground, coming away from her thoughts, cursing at the sting of cuts on her palms. The time for worrying over why she was here was not now. *Now* was the time for running, for saving her skin; what was left of it to save. She'd fallen so often in the long, yet very short time since she started this race for her life. Once she caught her arm on the bark of a tree, tearing into her top and digging down until the sharp remains of wood pierced her skin. She'd cursed then, too, crying out at the pain, at the injustice of it all; filling the quiet night with the sounds of her protests. Her hands were now covered in shallow scrapes from rogue tree roots that had tripped her, and the rough ground that had caught her. There was no end to the sharp stings or dull aches that were blossoming all over her body. There was no end to the terror that bloomed through her chest, working her heart into a frenzy.

Tall trees loomed above Leanne, confusing her, making her think that she'd seen this tree before, the one that she was leaning against, panting. Was she going round in circles? Had she crossed her own tracks in an attempt to get away?

Her thoughts came faster and faster, working in sync with her lungs. In and out. Paranoia. Fear, in, out. There seemed to be no discernable difference between her waves of emotion and the heaving of her chest. They were one and the same, reminding her that she was running out of time. Running out of energy. *Running*.

A crash behind her spurred her forward. Pushing away from the bark, she no longer felt the sting in her palms, only the dread in her gut. He was catching up. She needed to *run*.

Legs pumping, breath still coming in gasps, eyes darting back and forth like a trapped animal looking for escape, she ran as fast as she could. Every step she took was a step away from *him*. Every step she took was a step in the right direction to saving her life. A life that she had thought was over when Kyle's hands first closed around her throat.

After reaching for him she'd backed away again, scared at the look of pure hatred etched into his face. He'd stayed still for but a moment; long enough for Leanne to think that she was imagining it all in the dark of the moonlit car. Long enough for her to feel the stirring in her stomach of a primal fear that was older than the night itself.

Slowly, as though he was trying not to scare her, Kyle edged forward, reaching for her. It was such a caring gesture; palms out and up. A completely innocent gesture; one that someone would use if they'd just scared the living hell out of the woman that they had proposed to.

But then the hands came up. Quick as a snake, precise as an arrow, they closed around her throat like a bear trap snaring its prey. Tight, tighter, suffocating her with their grasp. Fight or flight had kicked in just a second after her air supply had been shut off, making her struggle and fight against his grip, bruising her throat, making it even harder to breathe. Heart racing, she kicked out with her feet, lashed out with her hands, aiming for something, *anything* that would get him to loosen his grip. Leanne wasn't thinking about what was happening or why. All that was running through her mind was *get me out of here.*

She would have done anything to end it in those dark moments more stumbling than running from tree to tree. Anything at all, had the opportunity arose. But all that accompanied her through the night was the fear in her gut and the plague of heavy footfalls that sounded closer and closer.

Kyle should have been limping, struggling as he chased Leanne through the dense woods. She'd kicked him hard enough to daze him for a moment, the moment that had seen her springing from the car and starting on her race for life. But the footfalls that followed her though this nightmare were strong and even. They were the footfalls of someone who had *let* her get away. Someone who *wanted* her to run through the woods, fearing for her life, stumbling at each turn and trying to get away but never running far or fast enough.

Legs pumping. Heart racing. Thoughts as erratic as her breathing…

Finally!

Salvation loomed out of the darkness, filling her weak night vision with a sight that couldn't have looked better even if it had been bathed in the summer sun of a tropical beach, with sand and sea kissing like long lost lovers.

The dead tree looked better than anything she'd ever seen. No sight or heaven could compare to the hope that flared in her stomach, beating about like a herd of butterflies. She paused. Held her breath. Listened. The footsteps that were following her stopped just after she did, the sound bleeding away until only the living night remained. Her heart thudded in her chest, almost drowning out the loudest of nature's cries. It wasn't nature that Leanne was concerned about, however; it was footsteps, quiet and stealthy, that she was listening for.

Survival Instincts

Seconds seem to evaporate into minutes, and minutes felt like they were draining away to hours as she stood there, holding her breath in the deadly night.

Quiet as a mouse, Leanne moved forward, one step at a time, inching her way towards her only hope. With each new step she paused, listened, then moved again, only to pause once more. If this was her only hope, she was not about to take the chance of getting caught.

Please, she thought, *please let me survive this. Please let me live.*

Releasing the breath that she had been holding since stopping, Leanne stepped into the black gash of the tree trunk, letting it swallow her up into the night like a shadow. She reached back with her hand, blindly searching the space that she had, whilst keeping an eye out for her fiancé... no, her *attacker*. Kyle was no longer the man that she loved. He was the man that she would fear for the rest of her life if she survived. *When* she survived. He was the one who would haunt her dreams, stalk her thoughts, and always be waiting in the shadows of her nightmares, ready to force her to relive this moment time and time again.

Leanne's hand came into contact with something soft and warm, and she let out a sigh of relief. *It's moss,* she thought, eyes scanning the darkness, *just moss.*

She couldn't hear anything in the stillness of the tree trunk. All she could see was the darkness outside of her safe haven. Nothing moved. No footsteps followed her. Leaning against the back of the tree, she sighed. Just a breath of a sound, relief that she didn't have to run anymore, that she was *safe*.

Something wrapped around her waist.

Too startled at first, it had a good grip on her before the bone chilling scream worked its way up her throat and out into the night.

A hand clamped across her mouth, cutting off the scream, silencing her. Eyes wide, Leanne kicked and struggled, fought against him. Who else could it have been? He hadn't been following her, stopping when she had, crashing through the trees and stopping just seconds after she did. Those were *her* footsteps. *Her* crashes and falls, blunders and scrapes echoing in her own ears, making her feel like she was being chased.

A light blinded her, stripping away what little night vision she had and replacing it with the feeling of being caught. Trapped in the headlights like a helpless deer too afraid to run, rooted to the spot where only death lived, where he was waiting to welcome her with open arms.

Swift and accurate, Kyle grabbed her arms, pulling them taunt, snapping something around her wrists at her back, trapping her.

"HELP!" she screamed. "HELP ME!"

No one was around to hear. No one was coming to rescue her.

Something else was snapped around her ankles, making it impossible to run, impossible to get away. She was thrown onto her back, landing on the damp ground inside the tree with a smack. Kyle loomed above her, a smile plastered across his face.

"This is better," he said. "Much better."

"Why are you doing this?" Leanne asked.

Kyle just smiled at her, kneeling on the ground, straddling her waist and pressing against her body. He didn't answer her; just leaned in close, almost close enough to kiss her. Leanne shied away, twisting her body in an attempt to put some distance between them.

She closed her eyes, a tear sliding down her cheek. She didn't want it to end like this. She didn't want her life to come to such an abrupt end, secluded in the arms of the man she was supposed to marry. She wanted to *live*! To go back to work on Monday, to talk to people and see them smile as they told her of their holidays and plans.

But as she felt the pressure around her neck, she knew that there would be no Monday. There would be no more listening to people's tales of exotic holidays and family dramas. This was it. Lying on the cold, damp floor, inside what should have been her salvation, was where her life would end.

"Why?" she choked out, her lungs burning, body thrashing against the unstoppable tide of death.

This time he answered her. As Kyle pressed his fingers ever deeper into her flesh, cutting off her air, he granted Leanne's last request.

Survival Instincts

"Because you said yes."

He left her body on the floor, bound and cooling, with a smile on his face.

The Perfect Gift

As Jake stared at the mass of text on his screen, he idly wondered if anyone had ever read it all. Just one word matter to him: the one leading to a private login page. A few clicks and a password that changed daily, and Jake was in.

The boards were quiet, but the post he wanted sat blinking at the top with two edits under the large *New* sign.

Third name down was the group's 'Secret Santa' list was Matt. The man had specific interests, and gifts for Matt were always a challenge. The thought of it tugged at Jake's lips, twisting his face into a grin. He had three weeks to get everything in place. Rent a car, pack, find presents for everyone, and drive the couple of thousand miles to the cabin.

As Christmases went, celebrating in the middle of July was the way to go. No herds stampeding to get the last stuffed animal. One that would end up abandoned on the floor of some unappreciative brat.

Jake knew, however, that the purple octopus he had in mind for Phyllis would be well cared for and never tossed aside.

"Is this for your son?" the cute blonde inquired.

Jake smiled like the caring father he was. "No, it's for a friend. She collects them."

"Oh, well, better than coins or stamps, I suppose."

"Cheaper, too."

The pair parted on a smile, the purple toy peeking out the top of its bright gift bag.

Jake had always enjoyed shopping for other people, often spending hours working out the perfect gift for each of his friends. But this was a special group of people that required the utmost attention to details.

The Perfect Gift

Every one reflected the commitment the group had made to each other. A deep knowledge of each other that went beyond simple friendship.

With the final gift wrapped and secure in the car boot, Jake took to the road for the four day trip.

Miles of road flew beneath him as the car ate away the distance. This was the part he hated most. Each stop tightened Jake's shoulders. Overnight stops being the worse. Nowhere with drunken holiday makers. Nowhere with kids. Privacy and quiet were his top priorities.

Jake went out of his way to find off-the-beaten-track places to pitch his tent.

Every night he tended to the only living gift he carried. Water, food, a bit of fresh air. Its conspicuous nature meant it had to remain in the boot for most of the journey.

Surprise and presents went hand in hand. Showing up at the cabin with the main gift on show would spoil all the surprise.

As Jake approached the cabin, he saw that everyone else was there. Four shiny rentals lined up outside the wooden building, each as identical as the next. The precautions they took to keep this meeting secret, extended, as always, to every detail. Identical rentals was the tip of an iceberg large enough to sink any ship.

The solid wooden door swung open to reveal a slender brunette in shorts, a vest, and hiking boots.

"Jakey boy! Glad to see you made it."

"Did I have you worried, Phyllis?"

She stepped off the porch and wrapped her arms around Jake. "Never. So what did you bring me?"

Jake winked. "Wait and see."

The pair sauntered into the cabin where Matt, Bill, and Steve were lounging around a roaring fire.

"Am I *that* late?" Jake asked.

Steve rose in a lithe movement that brought him up to his almost-ceiling-reaching height. "Nah, mate, we got here early's all. Ya need a hand with ya stuff?"

"Just this." Jake held up his one packed bag. "Presents are in the car."

"Give it 'ere then. Ya sharing with me this year."

The guys paired up every year and took turns sharing with each other, leaving Phyllis the third bedroom.

Jake took Steve's seat, whilst Steve strode off with the case.

"How's life?" Jake asked.

"We're all here." Matt's grin split his face in two. "Doesn't get better than that."

Bill raised his beer in agreement. "Must say, I haven't seen any of you in the news this year."

"Ah, Bill, we don't all have your flare for the dramatic, you know," Jake jibed.

"Speaking of. Presents? We're all here, and I've been looking forward to this since last year's fun and games."

"Just waiting for an opening, weren't ya, Bill?"

Bill grinned at Steve. "You know me!"

"Not as well as you'd like, mate!"

"You're not my type."

"Boys, boys!" Phyllis said. "We going to flirt or open our gifts?"

Matt slapped his chair arms as he rose. "Gifts!"

The group rose and filed out into the late evening sun. Long shadows like dark fingers stretched out from the forest.

"Right, who's first?" Phyllis asked.

The four men chewed over who got to give their gifts first. Matt spoke first, "Last here, first gifts?"

The Perfect Gift

Jake didn't understand the logic, but he wasn't one to pass up the offer. Not when it meant he could get all the worry out of the way and enjoy getting his presents.

He rubbed his hands together and flung open the back door. Three gift bags in matching shades of blue lined the backseat.

"Ladies first," he proclaimed, handing the first bag to Phyllis.

She grinned as she peered into the bag and pulled out the stuffed octopus.

"I hope you've never had one before."

She clung the toy to her chest and glanced up at Jake. "This is fantastic."

When she looked back, she began pulled the tentacles this way and that, seeing in which positions she could hold them.

"It will take pride of place on my shelves," she commented. "When I'm finished with it."

Bill's gift was next. Nothing quite as exotic.

"Damn," Bill said, pulling the small, curved blade from the bag. "Never seen one of these before."

"Child-size, fully functioning Persian sword. Or so I'm told."

Bill grinned. "Cash payment, I assume?"

"On a day when the cameras were down and they had a sale on the whole shop. I know the rules." They all did.

Last small gift went to Steve. The bag pulled at its handles; Jake's hand hovered under it as he handed the weight over.

Steve peered into the bag. "Is this...?"

"Hand-polished slate, meant for water features and the like."

"Damn, mate, this is like Christmas all over again."

"Yeah, but postage on it's going to be a bitch."

Steve nodded. "Yeah, but I do love seeing their faces in the news."

They shared a laugh before Jake moved on to the final gist that remained in the boot of his car. He tossed the keys to Matt and swept his arms in an help-yourself gesture.

Matt approached the car with wide eyes and slow movements. He slid the key into the lock as carefully as if it was a virgin. His breathing quickened enough that Jake could see the breaths shuddering out of his chest as Matt flung the boot lid open.

Laid out inside was a very special gift of a very specific type. Twenty-four years old. Shoulder length black hair. Wide set eyes. And a figure any model would be jealous of. She stared up, blinking in the sudden light.

Matt reached down and stroked her cheek, making her flinch away from him.

"She's perfect," Matt whispered with reverence. "Just my type."

Jake watched Matt's admiration of his present and thought to himself, *Some things are better than Christmases.*

His wife and daughter always enjoyed the presents he got them, but never the way his friends did.

From Phyllis and her need to strangle abusive fathers with the ultimate image of childhood—stuffed animals.

To Steve, who enjoyed bashing in the heads of cheating girlfriends and then posting the murder weapon to their family.

Bill, whose preferences were limited to weapon of choice instead of victim.

And Matt, with a type so specific it took weeks to find the perfect gift.

Most would say Jake and his friends were sick in the head, twisted for their love of torture, torment, and death. To Jake, they were better than family.

The Perfect Gift

Never Go There

An autumn moon gave the abandoned school the look of a broken ghost rising from the weeds. No one knew how long the building had been rotting; long enough to warrant warnings pasted across its failing fences.

'Keep Out,' they read. 'Danger.'

Ollie and her friends snuck through the clinking fence, ignoring the warnings. Weeds whispered as they crept towards the derelict building.

"Not sure we should be doing this," Ollie said. She stared up at the building until her neck strained to see the crumbling roof.

"Sure we should!" Lee clapped Ollie on the back and ducked through a half-gone door.

His brother followed, leaving Ollie standing alone in the cold. One last look up sent a shiver down her spine that was less to do with the cold and more to do with the stories surrounding the place. It raced down her spine every time she looked at the building. Stories of how and why the school had come to be abandoned had been told for years. Everything from hauntings to monsters to bloodshed.

Ollie ducked under the broken doorframe. She gagged on a heavy, musty smell that reminded her of opening a fridge that hadn't worked in weeks.

Her friends had disappeared, but Ollie refused to call out for them. No doubt they would jump out from behind a half-open door just to see her leap through the ceiling.

With a shake of her head, Ollie set off down the wide corridor. Doors stood open, letting the moonlight light her path. A quick glance into the first room made Ollie pause. Sitting on the desks were dust and grime coated books. She stepped into the room and a breeze stirred leaves that had flittered in through broken windows.

A bag lay on the floor by the teacher's desk, contents spilled onto the dirty floor. The desk resembled every desk Ollie had seen during her time in school, right down to the mug sitting at one corner next to a stack of papers. She didn't dare peek inside in case something was still growing there.

Out of tune piano music drifted down the half, turning Ollie into an icicle.

"We found the music room!" someone shouted.

Relief flooded through Ollie, relaxing her to the point that she had to lean against the desk to keep from having an intimate encounter with the floor.

Lee trotted in. "Here you are. We found the music room."

Ollie muttered, "So I heard," and followed him out of the room.

Their footsteps echoed as they made their way to the music room. Ollie thought she heard something; a scraping against the wall. But when she looked, nothing was there but untouched dirt.

She followed Lee into the music room and paused. The room was filled with equipment. From the piano she'd heard earlier to guitars and flutes. A whole band was sat in the room, waiting to be cleaned, tuned, and played.

Gabe, Lee's younger brother, sat at the piano, poised and ready to play.

"I didn't know you played," Ollie commented.

"I don't."

Noise crashed out from his fingers, confirming that he had no idea what he was doing.

Lee grinned and sprinted across the room. He skidded to a stop behind the drums.

"Aha!" he proclaimed, holding a pair of sticks high.

Ollie clamped her hands over her ears.

"You sound like a bunch of kids with pots and pans!" she shouted over the noise.

Gabe ceased bashing the poor piano long enough to ask, "What?"

But when Ollie repeated herself Gabe had to turn to Lee and gesture for him to shut up. Silence gave way to ringing ears.

"I said, you sound like a bunch of kids with pots and pans." She stuck a finger in her ear, trying to dislodge the ringing sound. "And anyway, aren't we supposed to be exploring this place, not advertising we're here."

The brothers shrugged in unison and abandoned their instruments. Good job, too, Ollie thought. She wasn't sure how much more of the racket she could take.

The trio traipsed back into the corridor, the brothers taking the lead as they passed classroom after classroom in perpetual disarray.

"What happened here?" Ollie asked.

"No one knows. People say someone was murdered, and that the place is haunted."

Ollie shook her head. "Yeah, but that doesn't explain why it's so... full."

"Full?" Lee asked.

"With stuff. Mugs, papers, instruments. Someone should have stripped the place long ago."

Gabe shrugged. "Maybe they were scared away."

"Yeah, by your 'music,'" Ollie answered, complete with air quotes.

"She's right, though," Lee added. "Remember that hotel we lived near? It caught fire and no one rebuilt it. Within a month people had cleared the place out. Nothing left. Not even the carpets."

"So maybe the fence kept them out?"

Silence came in place of an answer.

Before them, the stairs rose like a broken tower from the ground. The handrail lay in a useless heap, but the stairs appeared intact.

"Up?" Ollie asked.

Lee grinned. "Why the hell not?"

"I can think of some reasons," Ollie muttered.

Starting with the lack of a handrail and the rubble dotting steps. Still, they were here, she thought, *might as well take the full tour*. At least no ghosts or monsters had crawled out of the walls to greet them, so maybe the stories were all superstition. It didn't stop a faint feeling of nausea invading her as they began their climb.

She expected the ancient stairs to creak under their weight, but the higher they got, the more solid they seemed. Temptation suggested Ollie jump on them, but sense won. Leaving alive was preferable.

Never Go There

As Ollie stepped onto the landing, a sound caught her attention. She glanced back and a shadow move in the dark. A quick blink and it was gone. Just her eyes buying into the mystery of the place before her mind could tell them to shut up.

Lee asked, "See something?"

"No." She shook her head and followed the guys along another identical corridor. One look and Ollie said, "Okay, this is getting boring. There's nothing here."

"That's 'cause we haven't gotten to the good part yet."

"More empty rooms?"

"Nope." Lee grinned. "The assembly hall."

Ollie sighed. "Let me guess, it's a big hall that's… empty."

"Where someone died."

"No, Gabe, get it right."

"Okay, okay, where the whole school died."

Ollie stared at her friends. "And that's nowhere to be found in any news source… because?"

"No one dared report it."

"Oh, for goodness sake." Ollie threw her hands up. "You two are ridiculous."

She stormed off, footsteps echoing. Lee and Gabe followed. They'd heard the stories, but didn't believe. Nothing had ever been reported, and no one seemed to know exactly how long the school had been desolate. All anyone old enough to remember would ever say was, "Never go there."

Tales surfaced of people trespassing and never returning, yet nothing ever made the news.

But as Ollie strode away, a sound halted her. Scratching. Gentle and quiet. Coming from the wall. Gabe and Lee caught up and started to speak, but Ollie shushed them and pointed to the sound.

"You hear that?"

They inched towards the wall together, leaning in as they listened. It stopped, and they looked at each other.

"Should we go in?" Lee asked.

Gabe straightened and went for the door. Lee grabbed for him but missed. Gabe threw open the door to the classroom and stuck his head in. He leaped back with a shout.

Ollie scurried to the opposite wall in hopes of getting away from...

"Ha! Gottcha!" Gabe laughed, one hand on the doorframe, the other holding his stomach. "It's just a rat."

The offending creature scurried out of the room and past Ollie, making her yelp.

"What's wrong, Ollie? Scared of a little rat?"

She picked up a discarded book, and threw it at the guys, both of whom were now laughing.

"You call that thing little?" The size of her head with a tail as long as her arm was *not* little.

"Hey, it ain't a ghost."

Ollie stood in the corridor, one hand on the wall, the other on her chest trying to keep her heart from breaking free. The noise had been the same as the one she'd heard downstairs. But if it was only a rat, then that was fine. Unfortunately, her mind wasn't convinced.

Stupid men and their stupid stories, she thought. Her mind was now buying into the same thing her eyes had claimed to see in the stairwell. Shadows, ghosts, monsters. None of them real, but Ollie's body conspired against her until she found it hard to breathe.

"Hey," Lee asked, "you okay?"

"I fucking hate rats," she spat.

Lee wrapped an arm around her waist and pulled Ollie close. They hugged for a brief moment before Gabe made noises about getting a room. The guy had always been immature, and this latest adventure proved it. Lee and Ollie were friends, nothing more.

"Come on," Lee said, "let's do this so we can go home."

They headed into the darkest part of the school. Where before open doors had let in the night's light, now the doors were closed and nothing but darkness lurked.

"We're getting close," Gabe said, his voice a poor imitation of some Halloween special.

Lee thumped him. "Cut it out."

"What? We are getting close!"

Never Go There

Ollie glanced behind her and saw the remnants of light clinging to the edge of the darkness, almost as though they were scared to venture any closer.

"You ready?" Gabe's voice was too loud for the dark.

Lee nodded.

Gabe pushed open the double doors at the end of the corridor. A creak sprang up that left Ollie cold and scared. The doors scraped against rubbish as they opened, turning the whole thing into a bad opening for a low-budget horror.

"And here," Gabe proclaimed in a low voice, "is the scene of the crime. Where all fifteen hundred students and teachers burned."

Now it was Ollie's turn to punch Gabe. "Really? If they burned to death, then where's the remnants of the fire?"

He shrugged. "No idea. It's just one of the stories."

"Yeah, and so are the axe murdering headmaster, pagan rites gone wrong, and human sacrifice stories, but I don't see any evidence of those, either."

"You realise we might be the first people here in years?"

Bright light pierced the black, making Ollie's eyes sting. Lee shone his touch around whilst Gabe dragged out two more from his coat.

He grinned. "We came prepared."

The room lit up in shafts that revealed rubbish and not a lot else. They came out onto the balcony, looking out over the empty hall below.

Unlike the classrooms, the hall was more fitting of a derelict building. Tables and chairs were strewn about, as if a large hand had swept through them in a fit of rage. Great gouges marked whole sections of the wood floor.

"That's so cool!" Gabe said. "It looks like something out of a movie."

"Yeah, which means it's not the best idea to go down there." But Ollie's voice of reason was overruled.

They took the stairs carefully, letting the light search out each step.

At the bottom, wood splinters littered the floor, broken away from tables, chairs, and the floor itself. Interspersed in the chaos were strands of rope or heavy string.

Ollie picked one up and examined it under her light.

"Hey, what do you think of this?"

Lee glanced over. "Dunno."

"Wonder what it's from?"

"Who cares?" Gabe called. "This is awesome."

Ollie wandered across the hall. She hadn't reached half-way before the scratching began.

"Bloody rats," Ollie muttered.

Except this scratching was louder, closer. But Ollie was stood a good twenty feet from the nearest wall. Twice the width of the corridors.

She shone her light around the rubble, hoping to catch a glimpse of the offending creature. Nothing jumped out. No fur balls with tails scurried about. She looked around for Lee and Gabe, and saw them standing, fixated on the stage.

"You see something?" she asked in a quiet voice.

Neither of them acknowledged that she'd spoken, so she picked her way through the rubble. With each step, she swept the light around, checking for rats.

The scratching grew louder the closer she got to her friends. No rat Ollie had ever seen been big enough to make that kind of noise. Not without a microphone.

Still they stood transfixed, lights pointed in the same direction.

"Guys?" Ollie had a feeling that they were messing with her again, but as she inched across the floor, that feeling gave way to butterflies doing the loop of death in her stomach.

Then she saw it. Her light caught the edge of something dark against the stage; dark and moving. Her whole body froze to the spot, tensing up as fear took control.

In the moment between deciding on fight or flight, she saw the first claw. The white was bright against dark fur, but Ollie's eyes were fixated on the sharp, pale point that scratched at the floor, beckoning.

A second paw as large as Ollie's head emerged from the dark.

Flight took over and propelled her body into a skidding turn.

Never Go There

"Run!" she screamed.

She took the stairs two at a time, and could have sworn her friends were behind her. She reached the top and swung her light down. Her friends were still standing by the stage.

The creature, more monster than rat, emerged. Dark brown fur blended into the darkness, with flashes of pink and white for paws. It rose onto its back legs and let out a shriek that made Ollie's knees go weak.

She ducked behind the balcony wall, hands over her ears, tears stinging her eyes.

A second shriek brought up her head. She peered over the balcony in time to see a second and third rat crawl out from the ruined stage.

She clamped her hand over her mouth in the hope that if she stayed silent, they wouldn't come after her.

Staying silent, however, couldn't stop her from witnessing as the first creature tore her friends' bodies apart. Claws tore through them, leaving her friends as nothing more than blood and flesh amongst the rubble.

Ollie was dead unless she got out of here.

Her light swung wildly as she ran out into the moonlit hall. She glanced over her shoulder, watching for dark shapes and bloody claws. Nothing. But her pace didn't falter.

Until she hit the stairs. Half-way down, the broken handrail tripped her. Hard stairs took her breath away.

The last thing she remembered was a muttering voice and the face of someone standing above her.

The cool sun of autumn woke Ollie from her sleep. She stretched under warm covers and cringed. Her whole body protested.

"Oh, good, you're awake."

Her mother's voice startled Ollie into sitting up. How did she get here?

Three pairs of eyes stared at her. Her mother, her father, and…

The memory of the night before came rushing back to her, along with a massive headache. Her friends. Giant rats. The abandoned school.

"Here you go." Ollie's mother handed her a glass of water and two tablets.

She swallowed them in one. "What happened? What were those things?" So many questions. "What happened to Lee and Gabe."

"They're gone," the strange man said.

"Gone?"

"Dead."

Ollie's breath whooshed out from her, leaving her gasping and on the verge of tears.

"You were lucky," the man said. "You should never have gone there."

Panic gave way to anger, and Ollie let it fill her.

"Shouldn't have gone there?" she demanded. "Those things should have been killed, not left there to… to… murder people!"

The old man sat on Ollie's bed. "We tried. Fifty years ago when they crawled out of the ground, we tried. Fire wouldn't touch them. They ate poison like food. Only reason they don't kill the whole town is because we allow someone up there occasionally."

Ollie's mouth hung open. "You *let* people go up there to be killed?"

"We have no choice." This from Ollie's mother.

"You knew where I was last night?"

She nodded.

"And you'd have let it have me?"

Ollie's mother turned into the arms of her father. He said, "We had no choice."

"So what happens now?" Scorn laced Ollie's voice. "You expect me to say nothing?"

The old man said, "No. They let you go."

"And that means?"

"They like you."

"Oh, joy, because all my life I wanted to date a giant rat."

Everyone in the room went silent. For a moment she thought her joke and been right.

Never Go There

"You can't be—"

"No," her mother interrupted. "No. But…"

"You are to take over when I die," the old man said.

"Take over what? Who are you, anyway?"

"I'm Jamill, and I've been looking after the school for fifty years, since they first emerged. Now it is your turn."

Ollie pulled her knees to her chest. "Hell no. How do you even know they liked me? I might have just been faster than they were."

Jamill shook his head. "Your friends were transfixed by the sight of them, as are all who venture there. You weren't. They never intended to harm you."

"This isn't happening," Ollie muttered. She turned onto her side, back to the room and repeated those words over and over to herself in the hopes this was a dream.

A decade later, and the nightmare lived on, as Ollie watched two more unlucky souls enter the old school. Ten years had passed since Lee and Gabe had fallen prey to the rats, and it was time they fed. For ten years Ollie had muttered the words she wished she'd listened to…

"Never go there," she would whisper. "Never… Never go there."

Other books by Michelle Birbeck

The Keepers' Chronicles:

The Last Keeper
Last Chance
Exposure (Coming in 2014)
Revelations (Coming in 2014)
A Glimpse Into Darkness: A Keepers' Chronicles Short Story

Novels:

The Stars Are Falling

Short Horror Stories:

Consequences
Isolation (Free ebook)
Survival Instincts (Free ebook)
The Perfect Gift (Free ebook)
The Phantom Hour
Playthings

About the author

Michelle has been reading and writing her whole life. Her earliest memory of books was when she was five and decided to try and teach her fish how to read, by putting her Beatrix Potter books *in* the fish tank with them. Since then her love of books has grown, and now she is writing her own and looking forward to seeing them on her shelves, though they won't be going anywhere near the fish tank.

You can find more information on twitter, facebook, and her website:

Facebook.com/MichelleBirbeck
Twitter: @michellebirbeck
www.michellebirbeck.co.uk